BIRCHES

By Robert Frost
Illustrated by Ed Young

Henry Holt and Company
New York

When I see birches bend to left and right
Across the lines of straighter darker trees,
I like to think some boy's been swinging them.

But swinging doesn't bend them down to stay
As ice storms do. Often you must have seen them
Loaded with ice a sunny winter morning

After a rain. They click upon themselves
As the breeze rises, and turn many-colored
As the stir cracks and crazes their enamel.

Soon the sun's warmth makes them shed crystal shells
Shattering and avalanching on the snow crust—

Such heaps of broken glass to sweep away
You'd think the inner dome of heaven had fallen.

They are dragged to the withered bracken by the load,
And they seem not to break; though once they are bowed
So low for long, they never right themselves:

You may see their trunks arching in the woods
Years afterwards, trailing their leaves on the ground

Like girls on hands and knees that throw their hair
Before them over their heads to dry in the sun.

But I was going to say when Truth broke in
With all her matter of fact about the ice storm,

I should prefer to have some boy bend them
As he went out and in to fetch the cows—

Some boy too far from town to learn baseball,
Whose only play was what he found himself,
Summer or winter, and could play alone.

One by one he subdued his father's trees
By riding them down over and over again
Until he took the stiffness out of them,

And not one but hung limp, not one was left
For him to conquer. He learned all there was
To learn about not launching out too soon

And so not carrying the tree away
Clear to the ground. He always kept his poise
To the top branches, climbing carefully
With the same pains you use to fill a cup
Up to the brim, and even above the brim.

Then he flung outward, feet first, with a swish,
Kicking his way down through the air to the ground.

So was I once myself a swinger of birches.
And so I dream of going back to be.

It's when I'm weary of considerations,
And life is too much like a pathless wood
Where your face burns and tickles with the cobwebs

Broken across it, and one eye is weeping
From a twig's having lashed across it open.

I'd like to get away from earth awhile
And then come back to it and begin over.

May no fate willfully misunderstand me
And half grant what I wish and snatch me away
Not to return. Earth's the right place for love:

I don't know where it's likely to go better.
I'd like to go by climbing a birch tree,

And climb black branches up a snow-white trunk
Toward heaven, till the tree could bear no more,

But dipped its top and set me down again.
That would be good both going and coming back.

One could do worse than be a swinger of birches.

BIRCHES

When I see birches bend to left and right
Across the lines of straighter darker trees,
I like to think some boy's been swinging them.
But swinging doesn't bend them down to stay
As ice storms do. Often you must have seen them
Loaded with ice a sunny winter morning
After a rain. They click upon themselves
As the breeze rises, and turn many-colored
As the stir cracks and crazes their enamel.
Soon the sun's warmth makes them shed crystal shells
Shattering and avalanching on the snow crust—
Such heaps of broken glass to sweep away
You'd think the inner dome of heaven had fallen.
They are dragged to the withered bracken by the load,
And they seem not to break; though once they are bowed
So low for long, they never right themselves:
You may see their trunks arching in the woods
Years afterwards, trailing their leaves on the ground
Like girls on hands and knees that throw their hair
Before them over their heads to dry in the sun.
But I was going to say when Truth broke in
With all her matter of fact about the ice storm,
I should prefer to have some boy bend them
As he went out and in to fetch the cows—
Some boy too far from town to learn baseball,
Whose only play was what he found himself,
Summer or winter, and could play alone.

One by one he subdued his father's trees
By riding them down over and over again
Until he took the stiffness out of them,
And not one but hung limp, not one was left
For him to conquer. He learned all there was
To learn about not launching out too soon
And so not carrying the tree away
Clear to the ground. He always kept his poise
To the top branches, climbing carefully
With the same pains you use to fill a cup
Up to the brim, and even above the brim.
Then he flung outward, feet first, with a swish,
Kicking his way down through the air to the ground.
So was I once myself a swinger of birches.
And so I dream of going back to be.
It's when I'm weary of considerations,
And life is too much like a pathless wood
Where your face burns and tickles with the cobwebs
Broken across it, and one eye is weeping
From a twig's having lashed across it open.
I'd like to get away from earth awhile
And then come back to it and begin over.
May no fate willfully misunderstand me
And half grant what I wish and snatch me away
Not to return. Earth's the right place for love:
I don't know where it's likely to go better.
I'd like to go by climbing a birch tree,
And climb black branches up a snow-white trunk
Toward heaven, till the tree could bear no more,
But dipped its top and set me down again.
That would be good both going and coming back.
One could do worse than be a swinger of birches.

Text copyright 1916 by Henry Holt and Company, Inc., and renewed 1944 by Robert Frost
Illustrations copyright © 1988 by Ed Young
All rights reserved, including the right to reproduce this
book or portions thereof in any form.
Published by Henry Holt and Company, Inc.,
115 West 18th Street, New York, New York 10011.
Published in Canada by Fitzhenry & Whiteside Limited,
195 Allstate Parkway, Markham, Ontario L3R 4T8.
Library of Congress Catalog Card Number: 87-46359
Library of Congress Cataloging in Publication Data is available.

ISBN: 0-8050-0570-6

First Edition

Designer: Jeffrey L. Ward
Printed in Italy
1   3   5   7   9   10   8   6   4   2

ISBN 0-8050-0570-6